FRANKIE VS. THE PIRATE PILLAGERS

ALSO BY FRANK LAMPARD

FRANKIE'S MAGIC SOCCER BALL

FRANKIE VS. THE PIRATE PILLAGERS

FRANK LAMPARD

SCHOLASTIC INC.

ISBN 978-0-545-66612-1

Published by Scholastic Inc., 557 Broadway, New York, NY 10012, by arrangement with Little, Brown Books for Young Readers. SCHOLASTIC and associated logos are trademarks and/or registered trademarks of Scholastic Inc.

12 11 10 9 8 7 6 5 4 3 2   15 16 17 18 19/0

Printed in the U.S.A.   40
First printing, May 2014

To my mom, Pat,
who encouraged me to do my
homework in between kicking a ball
all around the house, and is still
with me every step of the way

Welcome to a fantastic
fantasy league — the greatest
soccer competition ever held in
this world or any other!

You'll need four on a team,
so choose carefully. This is a lot
more serious than a game in the
park. You'll never know who your
next opponents will be, or where
you'll face them.

So lace up your cleats, players,
and good luck! The whistle's
about to blow!

The Ref

CHAPTER 1

"Should we go in, too?" Frankie asked. "Maybe Louise got lost."

"Nah," said Charlie, glancing toward the haunted house. "She'll be out soon."

Frankie and Charlie were standing by the exit, waiting for their friend

Louise. The sun was dropping behind the Ferris wheel, and soon the carnival would be shutting down for the year and leaving town.

"Not scared, are you?" said Frankie.

Charlie blushed, and all his freckles stood out. "Of course not."

Frankie grinned. He remembered that Charlie hadn't wanted to go in last year, either. It *was* pretty scary. There were walking skeletons, dangling spiders, and wailing ghosts. He would have gone in again today with Louise, but it cost a dollar and he only had fifty cents left.

Frankie's dog, Max, was sniffing around the ground looking for scraps of food.

"Here you go, boy," Frankie said. He reached into his pocket and pulled out a dog biscuit. Max opened his mouth and Frankie dropped it in, then tickled the dog under his furry white muzzle.

The doors opened and a few screams drifted over. Then a balding man with pale skin and wide eyes stumbled out. It was their gym teacher, Mr. Donald.

"Looks like Donaldo's spooked," said Frankie.

Mr. Donald saw them and walked

4

over, smoothing down the few hairs on his head.

"Is that a spider on your shoulder, sir?" asked Charlie.

Mr. Donald jumped about a foot in the air, craning his neck.

"Only joking, sir," said Charlie.

Mr. Donald stared at them with a frown. "I hope to see you both at soccer practice tomorrow."

"Of course, sir," said Frankie. "We wouldn't miss practice for anything!"

Mr. Donald walked off, still checking his shoulder.

The doors of the haunted house creaked open again and Louise emerged. She was playing a handheld video game.

"We thought a skeleton might have gotten you," said Frankie.

Louise rolled her eyes. "*Sooo* not scary — I almost fell asleep."

Frankie checked his watch and saw it was nearly a quarter to five. "We should go home — my mom wants me back by five thirty."

"Mine, too," said Louise.

They made their way past the bumper cars and the ring toss. Their friend Kobe from school was standing behind a rope, trying to knock the tin cans off their stands with baseballs.

"Over here, Kobe!" said Charlie. "Hit me!"

Kobe turned and launched a throw toward Charlie. Charlie dove and caught the ball in his goalie gloves.

Max barked excitedly.

"The best goalies are —" Charlie began.

"— always ready!" said Frankie and Louise. They'd heard it a gazillion times.

Charlie threw the ball back. He *never* took his gloves off, except when the teachers forced him to. He said he even slept wearing them. Charlie might have been small, but Frankie knew he was the best goalie in their grade at school. Probably better than anyone in the grade above, too.

"Win any prizes, Kobe?" asked Frankie.

His friend shook his head. "Nope. I've hit the cans, but they don't fall off. Watch."

He crouched like a baseball pitcher and hurled a ball. It smashed right into a can that didn't even wobble.

"Better luck next time," said the short woman in a woolly hat and thick coat behind the game's counter.

"I bet it's fixed," huffed Kobe.

"Watch what you say, young man," said the woman. "I'm as honest as they come. Straight as an arrow."

But Kobe was already hopping over the rope toward the cans. He grabbed one and tried to tug it from its holder. "See!" he said. "I knew it — you're cheating!"

"Must be the hot weather," said the woman, folding her beefy arms. "It's made the cans stick together."

"I don't think that's true," said Frankie.

"Cheater!" said Louise.

"Cheater!" echoed Charlie. Max began to bark.

The woman shuffled over and put her fingers to her lips. "Keep it down, will you? Here!" She snatched a large pink teddy bear down from a peg and thrust it toward Kobe. "Take this and go."

Kobe looked at the bear with a frown. "My sister might like it. See you at school, guys."

As Kobe strolled off with his prize, Frankie and his friends walked toward the exit. The cheating woman had left a sour taste in Frankie's mouth. He hated when people didn't play fair.

Behind the hot dog stand, another booth caught his eye. It had a painted sign with a soccer ball whizzing through the air. *How come I didn't notice it earlier?* Frankie wondered.

"Hang on, guys," he said, walking over.

Max lingered for a moment, staring up at some hot dogs turning under a heat lamp.

"Come on, Max," said Frankie. "You'll get your dinner later."

At the soccer booth, an ancient man with bushy gray hair was up on a ladder, about to take down the sign.

"Is it too late to play?" Frankie asked.

The old man shook his head as he climbed down the ladder. "I'm afraid . . ." When he saw Frankie he paused, then nodded. "I suppose one more won't hurt. Fifty cents gets you three shots. Get it in the bucket and you win a prize."

He reached under the counter and pulled out a soccer ball. It must have been almost as old as he was. The ball was half flat, and the leather was cracked and peeling off.

He set it down in front of Frankie. Max sniffed at it, then whined.

"That bucket is tiny," said Charlie. "It might be fixed like the other game."

Frankie stared at the old man. There was something odd about him, with his eyebrows like bristling caterpillars and his deep wrinkles, but he looked honest enough. Frankie fished his last fifty cents out of his pocket and put it on the counter. He took a step back and drew in a breath. With a stab of his toe, he sent the ball sailing over the top of the bucket.

"Just missed," said Louise.

The old man placed the ball back at Frankie's feet. "Two tries left."

Frankie looked at the bucket, fixing it in his mind. This time he chipped the ball into the air with less power. He heard his friends all suck in their breaths.

The ball dropped toward the bucket, bounced off the rim . . . and onto the ground.

"Close," said the man running the game, "but not close enough." He brought the ball back again.

"Told you," said Charlie. "I doubt the ball even fits."

But Frankie didn't like to give up. He closed his eyes and told himself to relax.

"You can do it, Frankie," whispered Louise.

Frankie opened his eyes, took a step, and kicked the ball. It spun as it

rose through the air, then looped
down. It plunked right into the center
of the bucket.

"SUPERGOOAAALL!"

yelled Frankie, throwing his arms in
the air.

"Great shot!" said Charlie, clapping

him on the back. Max jumped up on his hind legs.

The old man rubbed his chin, his mouth gaping. "Well, I haven't seen a kick that good in years," he said.

Frankie smiled and blushed.

"What's the prize?" asked Charlie.

The old man looked at his feet. "Um . . . I don't have one."

"Huh?" said Charlie.

"Well, no one usually wins," he said. He looked Frankie right in the eye and held his gaze. "Tell you what, you can have the ball if you'd like."

"Oh, great," grumbled Louise. "Even Max wouldn't touch it."

But Frankie nodded. He wasn't sure why, but something drew him to the battered soccer ball.

The old man picked the ball out of the bucket and tossed it to them.

Frankie caught it on the arch of his foot and balanced it perfectly. "Must be my lucky ball," he said.

"You never know," said the old man, with a twinkle in his eye. "It just might be. Here, you'd better have this back."

The old man flicked the two quarters over. Before they reached

Frankie, Charlie's hand shot out and grabbed them. "Always ready," he said.

Frankie laughed. "Come on, let's go."

CHAPTER 2

"Do we have time to kick the ball around?" asked Louise, nodding to the park gates across from the carnival.

Frankie checked his watch. Five fifteen. *There's always time for soccer,* he thought. "Maybe for ten minutes."

They ran into the park. At first, Frankie thought it was completely empty. Then a voice called out, "Look who it is, Kev!"

Frankie turned around and saw his brother, Kevin, with two of his friends. They were leaning against a fence, drinking cans of an energy drink.

"Cool ball, Frank*enstein*," said Kevin. He laughed at his lame joke, downed his drink, then dropped the can on the grass.

"Let's get out of here," muttered Charlie.

But Frankie's blood was boiling. "You should put that in the trash, Kev," he said.

"Oh yeah?" said his brother. "You gonna tell Mom?"

Frankie stared at him. He knew that if their mom could see what Kevin had done, she'd drag him home by his ear.

Frankie walked toward his brother, then stooped to get the can. If Kevin wouldn't put it in the trash, he would. But at the last moment, his brother kicked the can out of reach. "Nice try," he chuckled. Frankie reached again, and Kevin dribbled it away, laughing. "Too slow, Frankenstein!" he said.

"That's enough," said Louise.

Kevin lifted his foot to kick the can

away. "Hey!" he shouted as Max charged in. The little dog snapped up the can in his mouth and ran off. Kevin lost his balance as he swung his leg and fell on his backside. Max trotted to a trash can, stood on his hind paws, and dropped the can in.

Frankie managed to keep a straight face, but Kevin's friends burst out laughing.

"Great skills!" said one of them.

"Tackled by a dog!" said the other.

Kevin clambered to his feet, blushing bright red. His jeans had a dark grass stain on the back. He turned angrily to Frankie. "You'd better not be late for dinner!" he said, and stormed off. His friends followed.

"Or what?" Frankie called after him jokingly. "You gonna tell Mom?" He gave Max another treat. "We'd better make this a quick game," he said to the others.

"There!" said Charlie, pointing to a jungle gym shaped like an old ship. He jogged over and stood in front of it. "The ship's the goal."

Frankie booted the ball high into the air. Max streaked after it. It tangled in his feet, and he tumbled over the top.

"Pass it!" called Frankie.

Max managed to nose the ball to Louise. She dribbled the ball in and out of the swings, then sent a curling shot toward the top corner of the goal. Charlie dove and just got his fingertips on the ball.

"Nothing gets past me!" said Charlie.

We'll see about that . . . thought Frankie. He got the ball and passed it to Louise. She looked up, ready to shoot, then stepped over the ball and flicked it up with her heel. Frankie was ready. He brought his foot around and connected with a perfect volley. The ball screamed toward the goal. Charlie leapt sideways, gloves open, but the ball passed beneath his outstretched hands. Frankie slid onto his knees, thinking his mom would kill him when she saw the grass stains.

"SUPERGOA . . ."

The shout trailed off in Frankie's throat.

The ball had vanished, and so had the ship. Max growled quietly. Frankie stood up, his heart thumping. He couldn't believe his eyes.

Where the goal had been just a second before was a swirl of light like nothing he'd ever seen. Colors flashed and spun in a disc shape, six feet across. He looked at Louise. Her jaw had dropped open.

Charlie picked himself up, bashing the ground with his fist. He still hadn't seen the spinning circle of light behind him. "I was so close!" he said.

"Um, Charlie," said Louise. "You might want to turn around."

He did as she told him, then leapt backward. "Holy moly! What is that thing?"

Frankie and Louise went to Charlie's side. The lights shifted and shimmered like oil on water.

"I have no idea!" said Frankie. "But it has to be because of that soccer

ball. I knew there was something weird about that booth where we won it."

He reached toward the . . . the . . . whatever it was.

"What are you doing?" asked Charlie.

Frankie turned to his friend. "My ball's in there somewhere," he said. "I have to get it back."

"Are you crazy?" said Charlie.

Frankie grinned. "It's just like when it goes into Mrs. Pratchett's garden."

Mrs. Pratchett was Frankie's grumpy next-door neighbor. There was only one thing she hated more than slugs in her garden, and that was Frankie's soccer ball.

"This isn't the same thing," said Charlie.

"Anyway," said Frankie, "it's gotta be my lucky ball. I got it past you, didn't I?"

Charlie mumbled something about being lucky. Frankie stepped closer. He swallowed as his hand passed through the surface of the swirling colors. "It feels warm." He held out his other hand to his friends. "Who's with me?"

"I am!" said Louise right away. She gripped Frankie's hand.

Charlie shook his head. "I hope I don't regret this." He took Louise's other hand in his gloved one.

Max nuzzled at Frankie's ankle.

Frankie took another step, and his arm slipped into nothingness up to his elbow. His skin tingled all over, as if electricity was passing through his whole body. "Now or never," he said.

Something gripped his arm and sucked him in.

CHAPTER 3

"What . . . wow . . . WHOA!"

Blackness swallowed Frankie. He felt his body toss from side to side. The others cried out in alarm. Louise's fingers clutched his tightly as he turned upside down. Colors swirled all around. Frankie found himself hurtling down a rainbow-colored chute feetfirst. He'd been on plenty of roller coasters in his life, but this was something else. He lost his grip on Louise as he spun around, headfirst, on his back, on his stomach, on his side. It was like a waterslide, but without any water, and much, much quicker.

Frankie managed to steady himself as he looped around a bend. In a flash, he saw the others shooting along behind him, limbs flailing.

"Uh-oh!" called Louise, her eyes staring past Frankie.

He turned and faced the way he was traveling. His heart thumped in panic. Ahead, the tunnel seemed to

disappear as it turned downward. Frankie scrambled against the walls, but they were more slippery than wet grass. He couldn't slow himself down.

"SORRRYY!" he cried as he plummeted over the ledge.

The chute was bottomless, and he tumbled down, wind rushing in his hair. Then he saw something. Wooden boards, rushing toward him. *This is it,* he thought, bracing himself. *This is the end. . . .*

The impact never came. All was dark, until Frankie realized he had his eyes closed. He was on his back, lying on a hard surface. The world seemed to rock beneath him and something wet touched his face. When he opened his eyes, he saw Max's furry face close to his, tongue lolling. Above him was a clear blue sky. A flag with a skull-and-crossbones design flew from a mast. A seagull screeched overhead.

A seagull? But we're nowhere near the ocean. . . .

Frankie sat up and gasped. He was sitting on the deck of some sort of old ship. There were wooden boards and poles everywhere. Huge, thick ropes trailed from the sails into big coils below. Beyond the rails, at the edges of the deck, dark blue water stretched in every direction. A salty smell filled his nostrils.

The others were picking themselves up, too, and looking around in wonder. Frankie was glad to see no one was hurt, but they definitely looked strange. Louise was dressed in a black skirt cut off just above her knees and a purple shirt. Charlie wore red shorts, a salt-stained blue jacket, and a polka-dotted bandanna. Frankie looked down at himself and saw similar clothing: dirty blue shorts and a striped sailor's top. He reached up to his head and pulled off a crushed-velvet hat with gold trim.

"We're at sea!" said Charlie. As he took a step back, there was a crunch, and he looked down. Frankie saw Louise's video game under his foot.

"No!" cried Louise. She crouched beside him. There was a huge crack across the screen. "It's broken!"

"I didn't mean to," said Charlie.

Louise shook her head. "My dad will be so mad. He's always telling me not to take it out of the house."

Frankie put a hand on her shoulder. "It might still work," he said.

Louise pressed a switch on the side of the player. Sparks shot out of the device, and she dropped it back onto the deck. "Oh!" she cried.

The player twitched on the ship's deck and the screen glowed. Rays of light shot out of the screen, then spread out into the hologram of a man. He wore a tight-fitting white T-shirt and shorts like a soccer referee. A whistle dangled around his neck. He turned to Frankie, and his image flickered.

"Greetings!" he said. "Welcome to the fantasy league. What is your team's name?"

"What?" said Frankie. He thought the man looked familiar.

The referee checked his watch. "No time for warming up. You have

been selected to play in the fantasy league. Team name, please."

"Frankie's FC!" said Louise. "Like the professional teams. Soccer is called 'football' in some other countries. The really famous teams are called 'football clubs.' FC, get it?"

"Hang on. . . ." said Frankie.

"Your ball, your team," said Charlie.

"So be it," said the Ref. Frankie felt a slight buzzing on his chest. When he looked down, an emblem had appeared there, with "FFC" written in an upside-down triangle.

"Cool!" he muttered.

"Frankie's FC," said the Ref. "Your first match is against the Pirate Pillagers."

"Pirates?" said Frankie. So that's what the skull and crossbones meant.

"Right ye are, me hearties," said a voice.

Frankie and his friends spun around. A man wearing a tattered

red jacket stood before them. In place of one of his legs was a wooden peg. His straggly brown hair looked like it needed a lot of shampooing, and he had a thick patch of stubble on his chin. At his side, he wore a cutlass.

"Who are you?" asked Louise.

The pirate limped forward, his wooden leg knocking on the deck. Frankie noticed that the buttons on his jacket were the shape of miniature soccer balls. "I be Captain Cropper, owner of this vessel, *The Jolly Striker*, and I think ye stowaways have come to steal my treasure."

"Actually, we just came to get our ball back," said Charlie.

The captain scowled. "Yer ball, ye say! Well, what about *that*, Rolf?"

The deck creaked as a huge man emerged wearing an open leather shirt. He must have been seven feet tall, with tattoos covering his barrel chest, and a hook for a hand. In his other hand, he gripped the magic soccer ball. "Looking for this, are ye?"

Frankie gulped and nodded.

A flash of color caught his eye as a parrot with red–and–yellow wings and a blue breast landed on the ship's wheel. It opened its beak and squawked, "This'll be easy! They're just kids."

"Did that bird just talk?" said Charlie.

"What's so weird about that?" said a gruff voice at Frankie's feet.

He looked down and saw Max staring at him.

"Did you just . . ."

"Sure did," said Max.

Frankie was still staring at his pet dog when a figure came swinging down on a rope. It was a girl, maybe a year older than them, with bright red hair and baggy turquoise pants. She landed lightly on the deck and bowed low to Frankie. "Scarlet's the name, and this 'ere parrot is Tito."

Captain Cropper sneered, revealing a couple of gold teeth. "So, landlubbers! Ready to face the finest team on the seven seas?"

CHAPTER 4

Louise laughed, then tried to cover it with her hand.

"Something funny, missy?" asked the captain.

"I just didn't know pirates played soccer," Louise replied.

Rolf growled and chucked the ball into the air. Tito the parrot swooped down and knocked it with his beak to Scarlet. She flipped onto her hands, caught the ball between her feet, and tossed it to Captain Cropper. He bounced the ball on one foot three times, then pinned it against the deck with his wooden leg.

"Yer in for a surprise, missy," he said.

"What's the prize?" asked Charlie. "And don't say buried treasure!"

The hologram of the Ref flickered above Louise's console. "The winners will get to play again."

"And the losers?" gulped Frankie.

Rolf extended his hooked hand

over the side of the ship. "The losers end up there — until they build a raft or the crabs eat 'em!"

Frankie squinted and saw a low, flat island, dotted with palm trees and not much else. *It's my fault we're here*, he thought. *There's no way I'm letting my friends get marooned on a desert island!*

"May the best dog win!" said Max, scampering back and forth.

Frankie swelled his chest and stepped up to face Captain Cropper. He held out his hand. "Let's start the game!"

Captain Cropper snarled down at the hand.

"Where is the goal?" asked Charlie. "Should we use the masts?"

The Ref shook his head. "Each game in the league has different rules."

Scarlet drew her cutlass and pointed to a tiny basket on top of the main mast. "The winner is the first to score three goals in the crow's nest."

"That's not how we play back home," said Louise.

"Not our problem," said Captain Cropper, throwing the ball onto the center of the deck. As soon as it stopped, a cannon blasted from the

51

side of the ship, making Frankie's ears ring.

"Ready?" said the Ref. He brought his whistle to his lips and blew.

Captain Cropper pounced toward the ball, and Frankie dashed in, too. He slid across the deck and reached the ball first, sending it between his opponent's legs. Frankie scooped the ball onto his foot and sent it curling into the crow's nest.

"Barnacles!" muttered the Captain.

"One—nothing, Frankie's team!" shouted Charlie.

"Beginner's luck!" squawked Tito.

The game restarted with another boom from the cannon, and again

Frankie closed in on the ball first. He barely heard Louise call "Look out!" before Rolf plowed into him. Frankie went tumbling across the deck like a bowling pin.

"That's a foul!" said Louise. "Ref?"

But the Ref seemed to have disappeared.

Rolf grinned at Frankie. "Nothing wrong with a little shoulder shove."

Max ran at the huge pirate, but just bounced off his leg.

We might as well try to tackle an oak tree! thought Frankie.

Rolf kicked the ball to Scarlet. With a swish of her leg, she chipped the ball into the crow's nest.

"One goal apiece!" said Scarlet.

"What are we going to do?" Charlie said.

Max's ears pricked up. "We need to stop chasing our tails."

Charlie rubbed his forehead with a gloved hand. "I can't believe I'm taking advice from a dog."

As the cannon sounded, Frankie sprinted toward the ball. Rolf charged in again, but Frankie stalled, then stepped nimbly past him. Captain Cropper was closing in, so Frankie passed the ball to Louise. As she steadied herself to shoot, Scarlet came swinging down on a rope.

Louise looked up, and bounced the ball off the bottom of a mast. It rolled to Max's feet.

"Shoot!" yelled Charlie.

"Knock it in!" called Louise.

Max took a few steps back, spun on the spot, and kicked the ball with his hind legs. It bounced off a barrel and flew up toward the crow's nest. He wagged his stubby tail in triumph.

It's going in. . . . thought Frankie. *He did it!*

Just as the ball hovered over the goal, Tito flapped into view and batted it with his wing.

The ball spun over the edge of the ship and landed with a splash.

"Drats and cats!" barked Max.

Everyone ran to the deck rail.

"Our throw-in," said Louise.

Frankie saw the water churning with dozens of triangular fins. "Sharks!" he shouted. One of the deadly creatures broke the surface of the water.

"If they eat the ball, we can't get home!" said Charlie.

But instead of swallowing the ball, the shark nosed it out of the water. Another one batted it into the air. A third thumped the ball with its tail.

"I guess sharks like soccer, too!" said Frankie.

"Either that, or they don't like the taste of leather," said Charlie.

After passing it back and forth among themselves, one of the sharks flicked the ball back toward the deck, over their heads. It stopped in mid-air, right on Rolf's hooked hand.

"Handball!" yelled Frankie.

"It's not my hand," Rolf sneered. Drawing back his arm, he tossed the ball into the crow's nest. "Two—one to the Pillagers!"

CHAPTER 5

Frankie's team gathered around him. "They're better than they look," he said.

"I feel seasick," said Charlie.

"They're nothing but cheaters, with all those fouls!" said Louise. "Where is the Ref?"

Frankie glanced around. The Ref

was lying in a hammock strung from the mast. He seemed to be asleep. "I don't think we'll get much help from him," Frankie said. Behind the hammock, the island looked closer than before, but no more inviting. How long could they last there without food or water?

"Maybe if we had a better goalie, we wouldn't be losing," muttered Max.

"There aren't even any goalposts!" said Charlie.

"Enough!" said Frankie. He hated seeing his teammates arguing with one another. "We're going to lose unless we play as a team."

"Frankie's right," said Louise. "I don't plan to lose to a bunch of smelly pirates."

"Maybe we need to cheat, too," said Max. "I could always give one of them a little bite on the ankle — slow them down a little."

"No!" said Frankie.

"I'm just saying," said Max, "it might even things up."

"We're not going to stoop to their level," said Frankie. "We play fair."

He peered over his shoulder. Captain Cropper had his foot up on the deck rail, doing stretches. He flashed Frankie a wide grin. Rolf was showing Scarlet the tattoos on his bulging arms, while Tito stabbed at what looked like a cracker with his beak.

I bet they've never lost before, thought Frankie. *That's their weakness. They're overconfident.*

"Look, team," he said. "Remember what Mr. Donald says when we play away from home?"

"Take off those gloves when you're on the bus?" said Charlie.

No one laughed except for Max, who gave a doggy chuckle.

"Not that," said Frankie. "He says, 'The field might look different, but the game's the same.'"

"This field looks *very* different," said Louise. "How can we even score? They've got a flying goalie!"

"I might not be able to fly," said Charlie, "but I'm not useless!"

Frankie huddled closer, and patted his pocket. "We need to distract Tito," he said. "And I've got just the thing." The others listened closely as he explained.

"It's worth a try," said Louise.

"Get a move on!" bellowed Captain Cropper. "I've seen sea slugs move quicker than you lot!"

They turned to face the Pillagers.

Rolf, Tito, and Scarlet were lined up behind their captain. Captain

Cropper hooked his thumbs in his belt. "About time," he said. "Decided which one ye'll eat first on the island?" He pointed to Frankie's dog. "That fella looks tasty."

"Don't count your treasure before it's dug up," growled Max.

The cannon fired and a gust of wind sent the smoke drifting back across the deck. Frankie coughed and wiped his stinging eyes, then ran at the ball. He saw the shape of Rolf closing in, so he slid the ball to Louise. She looked up to the crow's nest, as if she was going to shoot. Tito shot up from the deck and hovered, ready to stop the shot.

Frankie fished one of Max's dog biscuits out of his pocket and hurled it into the air. The parrot twisted midflight and swooped toward the dog treat.

"Now!" said Frankie.

As Tito snapped up the treat, Louise chipped the ball into the crow's nest.

"Two each!" Max barked.

The Ref suddenly sat up. "What . . . where . . . oh. Two goals a piece, is it? Then the next goal wins it." He shut his eyes again and began to snore.

"Oops!" said Tito, landing on the rigging.

Captain Cropper stamped his
wooden leg on the deck in anger.
"Birdbrain!" he growled. "I'll pluck
all of your feathers out if you fall for
that again."

"You said this would be easy,"
said Scarlet.

The captain narrowed his eyes and a smile spread across his lips. "Time for a change of course," he said.

Scarlet snickered and Rolf grinned, showing his black, rotting teeth.

Scarlet grabbed a rope as the captain crept closer to the mast. Rolf stamped toward the ship's wheel. *What are they planning?* Frankie wondered.

He looked across to his teammates. "Be ready," he said. "They're up to something."

Louise nodded and her eyes darted across the ship suspiciously.

"Where did Charlie go?" snapped Max.

Frankie shrugged. He couldn't see Charlie anywhere.

The cannon went off. For some reason, Captain Cropper didn't even move from the mast. He simply raised his hand. Frankie ran for the ball. He was almost there when Captain Cropper lowered his arm and gripped the mast. Rolf swung the wheel around violently and the ship lurched in the water. Frankie lost his balance and tripped. He saw Louise and Max go sprawling, too.

As he regained his footing, Frankie

saw Captain Cropper casually line up the ball. He gave Frankie a sly wink. "Bad luck, kiddies," he said, and kicked the ball perfectly.

Frankie stared in horror as it arced up toward the crow's nest.

It's all over. . . .

CHAPTER 6

Frankie saw a shadow behind the sail, near the top of the mast. It was too big to be Tito.

Then a gloved hand reached out and batted the ball away.

"Go, Charlie!" yelled Louise.

Charlie waved, then lost his grip.

He slid down the mast like it was a fireman's pole.

The ball landed on the deck and rolled to Max's feet.

"Tackle that mutt!" bellowed Captain Cropper.

Rolf thundered across the deck like a charging bull. The timbers shook under Frankie's feet.

"Shoot!" called Louise.

But Max looked terrified, frozen to the spot as Rolf bore down on him.

He's going to get squashed flat! thought Frankie.

Just as Rolf was about to crash into him, Max scampered to the side. The massive pirate flew into a barrel and toppled over the top. Max rolled the ball to Louise, but not hard enough. Scarlet and Louise reached it at the same time, and the ball went spinning through the air. It landed right beside Captain Cropper. Frankie was already running. He tipped the ball between the captain's legs, then took aim at the crow's nest.

I'll only get one chance, he thought. *Better not waste it.*

"Look out!" called Louise.

Frankie glanced up. Rolf was running at him, an enormous barrel raised over his head. His eyes were wild with rage and the deck creaked and groaned under him.

Uh-oh, thought Frankie. *I can score, but I'll get flattened!*

He looked left and right, then saw his chance. He fired the ball hard at a pulley coiled with rope. With a clunk, the rope began to unwrap and one of the large sails fell. Rolf was almost on him when the sail dropped over his head.

Frankie heard an "uh," then a mighty crash as the pirate tripped and hit the deck. The sail thrashed as Rolf yelled and writhed beneath it.

"Tito!" bellowed Captain Cropper. "Stop the ball!"

The parrot ruffled his feathers. "You called me a birdbrain," he said sulkily.

Frankie imagined he was back at the carnival with nothing more than fifty cents at stake.

He lifted his foot and swung. The wind caught the ball and it wobbled for a moment at the top of its arc. Scarlet tried to swing on a rope to stop it, but Max gripped the other end of it in his teeth. The ball rolled around the edge of the crow's nest, then fell in.

"SUPERGOOAAALL!"

Captain Cropper groaned and slumped to the deck.

Frankie's teammates piled on top of him, cheering.

"We won!" said Louise.

"Three—two!" said Charlie.

"I never doubted us!" Max yapped.

A loud whistle cut through the air.

As Frankie pulled himself free, he saw the Ref standing over the ball.

"Frankie's FC are the victors," he said. "I haven't seen a kick that good in years."

His words made Frankie pause. "I knew you looked familiar," he said. "You're the man from the carnival!"

The Ref winked. "I've been looking for a new team," he said. "Looks like I found one."

With a grinding sound, the ship suddenly shook from deep within, and leaned to one side. Frankie only just managed to keep his balance.

Rolf peered out from beneath the tangled sail. "We've run aground!" he said.

"You're marooned!" said the Ref. "Just as you requested."

"But — but —" stammered Captain Cropper.

"Don't be sore losers," said Louise. "Now, how do we get home?"

The Ref pointed across the deck, where a board hung out over the water. "Time to abandon ship," he said.

"You mean walk the plank?" said Frankie. He peered over the side. The water looked to be a long way down. And what about the sharks?

"Trust me," said the Ref.

"We don't have much of a choice," said Frankie.

He edged along the plank with Louise, Charlie, and Max behind him. When they were all standing side by side, he grinned at them. "Ready?"

"Yup!" said Louise.

"Maybe," said Charlie.

"No," said Max. "I hate baths, remember?"

"Until next time!" said the Ref.

Frankie leapt off the plank and felt gravity pull him down. He waited for the splash. . . .

Instead, he found himself sliding across grass on his knees.

"... GOOOAAALL!"

The ball bounced off the ship-shaped jungle gym beneath Charlie's outstretched arm.

The sun was still above the trees. The park was still empty. Louise was sitting on the ground, and Max was rolling over on the grass, scratching his back.

"Did anyone else just have the strangest dream?" asked Frankie. He looked down at himself and saw his normal clothes and sneakers.

Charlie picked up the ball and inspected it. "Um . . . sort of."

Louise held her video game in front of her. "Thank goodness! It's not broken anymore."

Frankie looked over at his pet dog. "Max?"

Max cocked his head, wagged his tail, but didn't say anything.

Frankie noticed something gleaming on the ground beside him. *My fifty cents? . . .* But when he picked it up, it was way too heavy. And it wasn't silver — it was gold!

A gold coin? Pirate treasure!

"Definitely not a dream," said Louise, peering over Frankie's shoulder.

"And definitely not the last time we play in the fantasy league!" said Frankie.

ACKNOWLEDGMENTS

Many thanks to Samantha Smith, Charlie King, Kate Webster, Madeleine Feeny, and everyone at Little, Brown UK; Neil Blair, Zoe King, Daniel Teweles, and all at The Blair Partnership; Mike Jackson for bringing my characters to life; special thanks to Michael Ford for all his wisdom and patience; and to Steve Kutner for being a great friend and for all his help and guidance not just with this book but with everything.

A SOCCER ADVENTURE IN ANCIENT ROME!

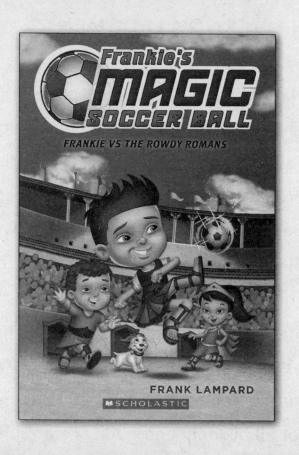

A SOCCER ADVENTURE OUT WEST!

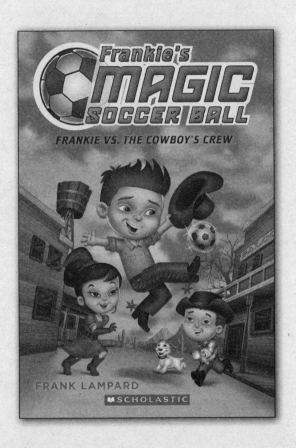

A SOCCER ADVENTURE IN EGYPT!